For Brenda, who showed me how
to enjoy the tiny things in life... (CH)

For Mum (SR)

Published by Trench Publishing, Manchester, UK

ISBN: 0992935199
ISBN-13: 978-0992935191

Stanley was at home, finishing off the best picture of a house he'd ever painted. He'd made a lovely job of the red bricks, the green hedges and the gigantic yellow robot he'd drawn in the garden pond. He only had to colour in the sky and he'd be finished.

He picked up the paintbrush and dipped it in the pot of blue paint but then stopped and looked puzzled.

He put the brush down and walked over to his Grandpa, who was sat in his favourite armchair, underneath a newspaper.

"Are you asleep, Grandpa?" Asked Stanley.

A spluttering noise came from under the newspaper.
"A-A-Asleep? No-no, I was thinking."

"But you were snoring,"
said Stanley

"Those were thinking noises."

"Grandpa," asked Stanley. "Why is the sky blue?"

"Stanley," replied Grandpa, sitting up in his chair, "I'm very glad you asked me that."

"Many years ago, when I was even younger than you are now, the sky wasn't blue like it is today. Instead it was a bright pink colour."

"Eurgh!" said Stanley.

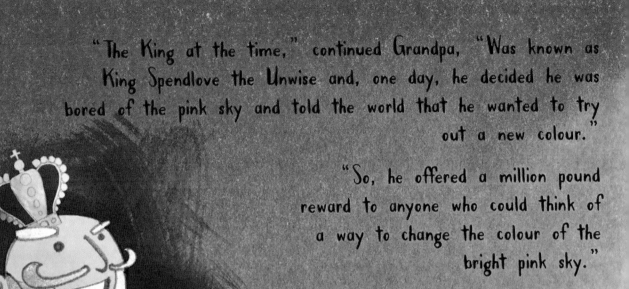

"The King at the time," continued Grandpa, "Was known as King Spendlove the Unwise and, one day, he decided he was bored of the pink sky and told the world that he wanted to try out a new colour."

"So, he offered a million pound reward to anyone who could think of a way to change the colour of the bright pink sky."

"And did many people bring along ideas?" asked Stanley.

"Oh yes! There were so many boffins and brainboxes trying to get into Buckingham Palace that they had to queue right the way round every single street in London," said Grandpa. "Twice."

"Some of them were tall and some of them were small; some of them had potions and some of them had lotions, but there was one thing that every single one of them had in common," said Grandpa.

"What was that?" said Stanley.

"They were all rubbish!" he laughed. "Absolute, copper bottomed nonsense! None of them came close to changing the colour of the sky, not even by a gnat's whisker!"

"King Spendlove had nearly given up on the whole scheme when, into the Throne Room, came the very last person in the queue."

"Who was it?" asked Stanley. "Another brainbox?"

"No." said Grandpa. "It was a clever little boy with an idea."

"Grandpa?" said Stanley.

"Yes, Stanley?" said Grandpa.

"Was the little boy called Stanley?"

"No. His name was Edgar," replied Grandpa.

"I see," said Stanley, looking a bit disappointed.

"Now then," said Grandpa. "Edgar was very nervous, stood all alone in the middle of that great big room, so when the King asked him for his idea, he just stood there, quiet as a mouse."

"After a few moments of silence, the King sat forward in his chair and frowned so hard you could hear his eyebrows bristle. He stood up and walked over to Edgar, then leaned all the way down and whispered in his ear, Nervous lad?"

"Was he nervous?" asked Stanley.

"Yes, he was," said his Grandpa. "He'd never even spoken to his Head Teacher before, let alone a King and he was very nervous indeed."

"But, King Spendlove was a kind-hearted soul and so he said, Don't be nervous. If you're feeling shy, you can whisper the idea in my ear."

"So Edgar leaned up on tiptoes and whispered his idea into the King's ear.

After a few moments, the King held up his hand for the boy to stop."

King Spendlove stood upright and marched slowly back to sit on his throne. The whole court sat waiting for him to give his verdict on Edgar's idea. Then finally, after what seemed like forever, he raised a hand and said in a loud, booming voice,

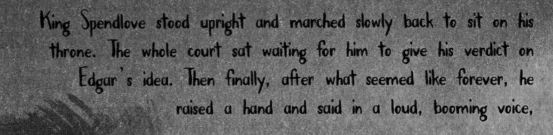

"This is the best idea in the history of the whole world!"

"Yay!" squealed Stanley. "Then the King smiled a great big smile and asked the boy exactly what he'd need to put his plan into action. Edgar pulled out a tatty piece of paper and began to read."

"First, he said, I need you to fetch me all of the biggest, loudest shouters in the world. Then, bring me ten million bottles of different coloured inks and fifty thousand brass trumpets."

"And how was all that going to change the colour of the sky?" asked Stanley.

"Wait and see," replied Grandpa as he picked up a biscuit from the arm of his chair and continued the story.

By next morning, the palace courtyard was packed full with thousands of bottles of ink, huge piles of trumpets and all of the biggest, loudest shouters in the world. There were scary maths teachers with spiky moustaches, circus ringmasters and Swiss yodellers... all ready to do their loud, shouty duty for the King. And among them, of course, were hundreds of old ladies. Because old ladies have the loudest voices of all."

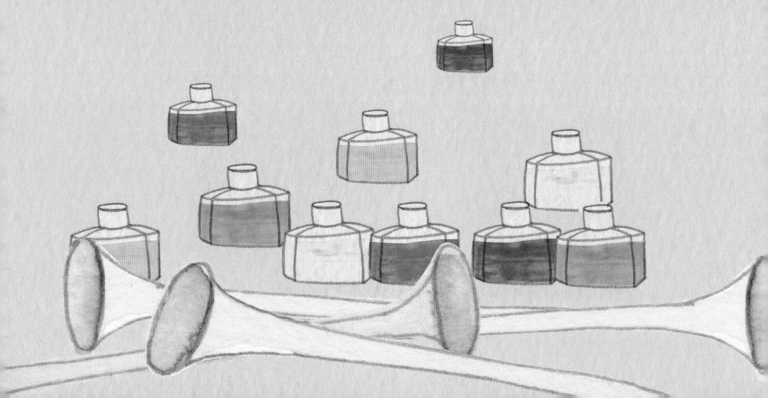

"Grandma hasn't got a loud voice," said Stanley.
"Try eating a cream cake before your dinner and you'll
see another side to your Grandmother," said Grandpa.

"Anyway, Edgar asked the King what colour he had chosen
for the sky. Green! boomed the King. So Edgar asked each
of the fifty thousand shouters to take a bottle of green ink
and pour it into the end of their trumpet.

Then in a clear voice, he said, When I count to three, raise your trumpets to the sky and blow as hard as you can. Are you ready?

"READY! they bellowed.

"OKAY, said Edgar. ONE... TWO... THREE!"

"Then," said Grandpa, "with a noise like a million elephants sneezing into a biscuit tin, the green ink was sprayed high up into the bright pink sky."

"What happened?" Stanley gasped.

"Nothing at first," explained Grandpa, "But after a minute or two, a few tiny spots of green appeared in the sky. And soon, those spots became bigger... and bigger... until slowly, they merged together and the whole sky was a beautiful green."

"But how did it work?" asked Stanley.

"Simple! It was the big, loud shouters that were Edgar's masterstroke. Their powerful lungs made the green ink shoot up past the clouds and soak into the sky cotton behind them.

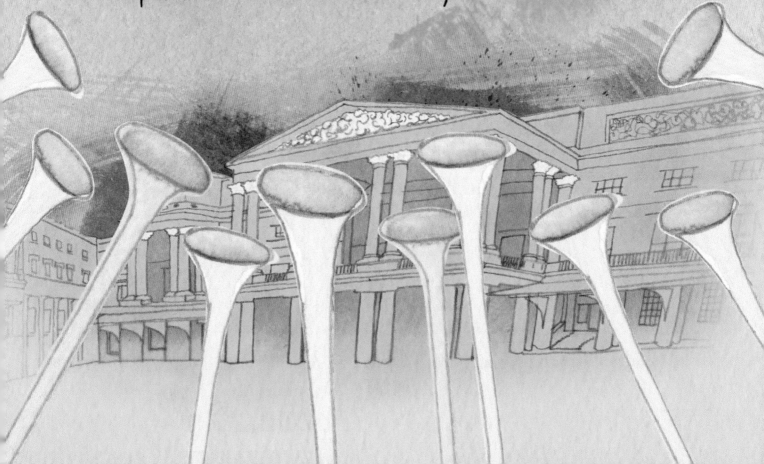

"Sky Cotton!? What's Sky
Cotton!?" whooped Stanley.
"Ask any qualified Scientist or
Space Wizard about sky cotton
and they'll tell you the same
as me! It surrounds the whole
planet like a big pair of net
curtains and stops the stars
falling on us at night."

"Are you sure about that,
Grandpa?" said Stanley.
"Of course I'm sure, now less of
your lip!" grumped Grandpa. "Now then,
for a while everyone enjoyed the new green sky, but after a few
weeks came a problem." "What kind of problem?" asked Stanley.

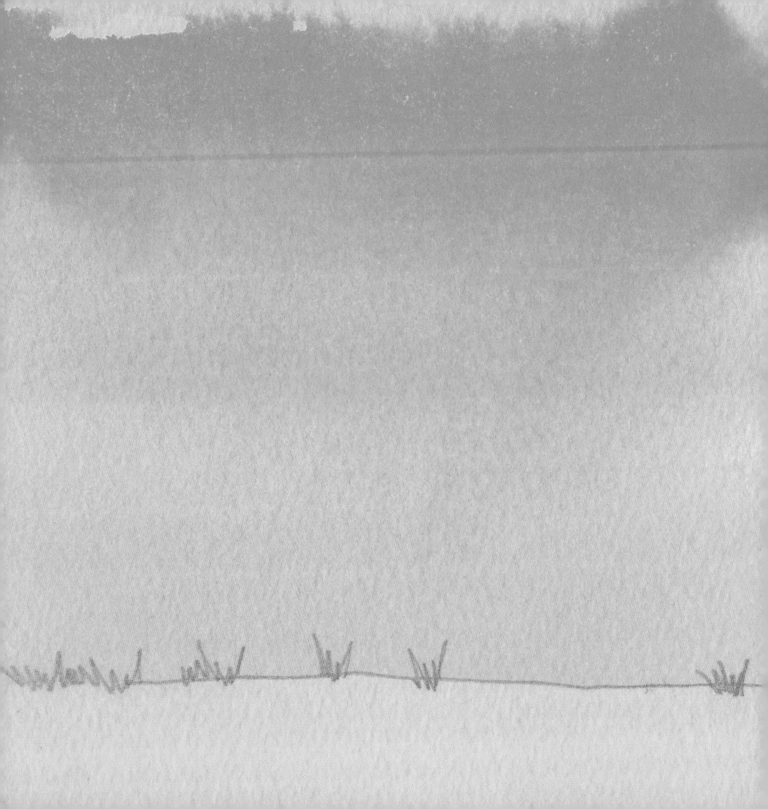

"The birds," said Grandpa. "Because all the fields were green, and so was the sky, they couldn't tell where the fields ended and the sky began.

"Uh-oh," said Stanley.

"Exactly. They kept flying head first into the grass and breaking their beaks."

"Oh no!" said Stanley, giggling.

"And then there were the cows," said Grandpa.
"A whole herd of cows walked over a cliff in Dover because they thought their field stretched on for miles. They landed with a colossal 'splash' in the sea and floated all the way across the Channel. They had to be rescued by a French lifeboat."

Stanley picked up a cushion and put it in front of his face.

"I do hope you're not laughing behind that cushion," said Grandpa. "Those poor cows ended up having to live in France. They had to learn how to 'moo' in French."

"So what did they do about the green sky?" asked Stanley.

"Well, King Spendlove commanded the biggest, loudest shouters to trumpet a new colour into the sky. And after thinking carefully, he chose dark brown."

"Sounds good," said Stanley.

"But it wasn't. It was too dark. Everyone kept confusing daytime for night. People were getting up when they should have been going to bed and going to bed when they should have been getting up."

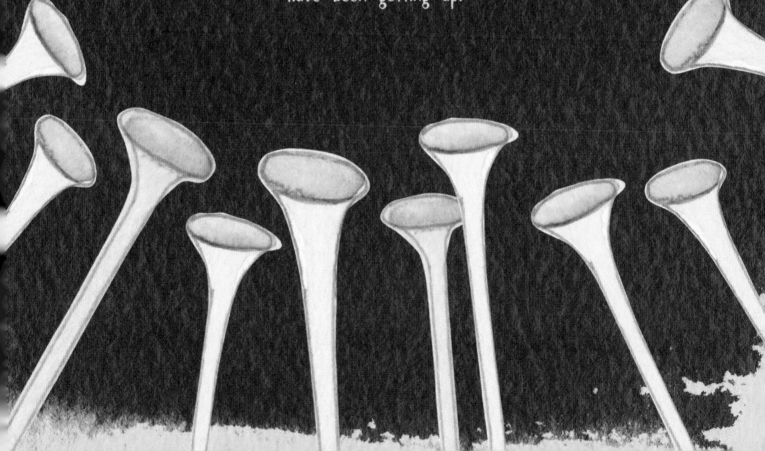

"So what colour did they try next?" Stanley laughed.

"A nice, bright yellow to cheer everyone up..."

"Did it work?" asked Stanley.

"Oh yes. Right up until they lost the sun."

"They lost the sun!?" hooted Stanley.

"Yes, because now it was exactly the same colour as the sky. It went missing for weeks! They thought they'd found it in North Wales, but it turned out to be a beach ball that had got stuck in a tree," giggled Grandpa. "After that, King Spendlove and Edgar tried a different colour for the sky almost every day."

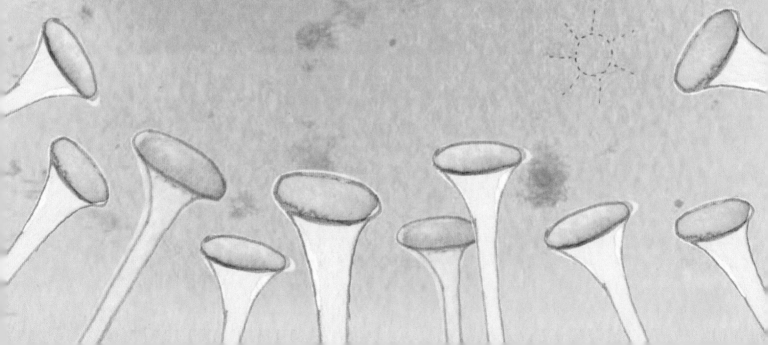

"Three months and seventy three colours later, Edgar and the King went down to the Ink Vaults to see what colours hadn't been tried yet. But disaster! No two bottles of the same colour were left on the shelves. So, in desperation, they fired all the different colours up into the sky at once."

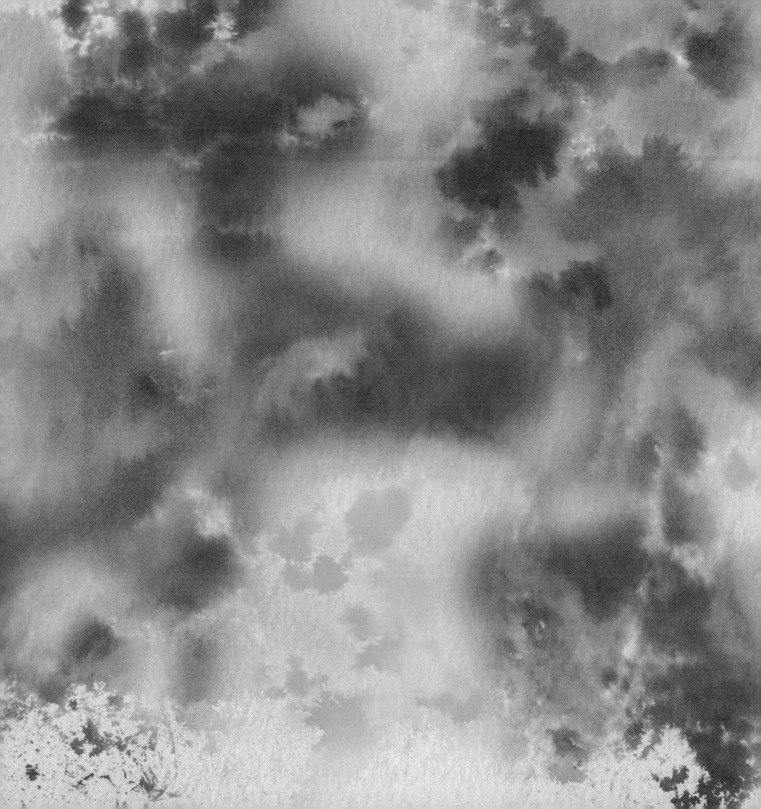

"And how did that look?" asked Stanley.

"Awful!" said Grandpa, "Like an explosion in a paint factory. And soon enough, everyone was barging into the palace, complaining and shouting things like, It's giving me a headache! And, it looks like cat sick!"

Poor King Spendlove cleared his throat, climbed up onto his throne and addressed the unhappy crowd, "Please, my people, I know that you're unhappy with the new sky. But I promise you, Edgar and I will work through the night to find a solution. If you all come back here tomorrow morning at dawn, we'll have thought of a way to fix everything. I guarantee it."

"So the King had a plan!" said a relieved Stanley.

"Nope." said Grandpa. "Neither of them had the faintest idea what to do. So after the crowds had gone home, they hurried inside and tried to think of a solution. All night long they racked their brains for the answer, but still they couldn't think of a way to fix the blotchy, splotchy sky.

Eventually, at three o'clock in the morning, tiredness got the better of them ... "

"But they hadn't thought of a plan yet!" said Stanley.
"The next thing they knew, they heard a rooster crowing, and they woke with a start."
"Oh no! said the King looking at his watch. It's dawn already. They'll all be waiting for us outside!"

"And no sooner had he spoken," said Grandpa, "Than they heard a crowd of people shouting outside the palace gates."
"What are we going to do? said the King, peering through the window. They're here already and we haven't got a plan or anything!"

"Edgar said calmly, 'Oh well, I suppose there's nothing left to do but go out and say sorry.'
"But listen to how loud they're shouting!' blubbed the King. 'They'll tear us limb from limb!'"
"By now, the crowd had begun to hammer loudly on the palace door and so they decided they'd better go out and face the music together. But, as they opened the door and stepped outside, they were greeted by the most astonishing sight they'd ever seen..."
"Instead of seeing the horrible, mixed up sky of the night before, they found themselves looking up at a beautiful, bright blue sky. And the people weren't angry at all! They were dancing and cheering and jumping for joy," laughed Grandpa.

"So who had fixed the sky?" said Stanley.

"No one!" said Grandpa. "It had happened all by itself!
During the night, all of the thousands of horrible colours
had run and spread and merged together on the sky cotton

to create a lovely, deep BLUE."
The people of the world were so thrilled with their new sky
that they had an enormous party to celebrate and they all
painted themselves blue from head to foot in honour of
King Spendlove and Edgar."

"Of course," laughed Grandpa, "King Spendlove pretended
that he'd planned the whole thing from the very beginning,
but no one really believed him."

"And what happened to little Edgar?" asked Stanley.

"Well, as a reward for his brilliant idea, he was made the King's Official Inventor. And he went on to invent all sorts of useful things, like Television, The Cat-flap, Custard Cannons and Zero-Gravity Football Boots."

"Grandpa?" said Stanley with a suspicious look on his face,
"Is that really why the sky is blue?"
"Why of course, Stanley," replied Grandpa with a grin.
"More or less!"

THE END

Printed in Great Britain
by Amazon